MY 1ST GRAPHIC NOVEL®

Down on the Farm

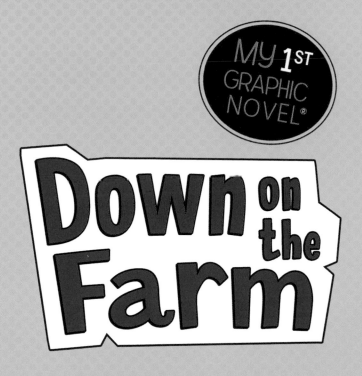

MY FIRST GRAPHIC NOVELS ARE PUBLISHED BY STONE ARCH BOOKS
A CAPSTONE IMPRINT
151 GOOD COUNSEL DRIVE, P.O. BOX 669
MANKATO, MINNESOTA 56002
WWW.CAPSTONEPUB.COM

Library of Congress Cataloging-in-Publication data is available on the
Library of Congress website.

ISBN: 978-1-4342-2516-0 (library binding)
ISBN: 978-1-4342-3063-8 (paperback)

Summary: Emily has always dreamed of riding a horse. When her dad takes her to a real farm, she
soon realizes she has to do chores before she can ride.

Art Director: KAY FRASER
Graphic Designer: HILARY WACHOLZ
Production Specialist: MICHELLE BIEDSCHEID

Photo Credits: iStockphoto: tacojim, 15; Shutterstock: Antonio Jorge Nunes, 7; Elena Elisseeva, 14;
Gregor Kervina, 9, 21; leonit_tit, 11; MWaits, 19; Nate Hall, 22 (bottom); Naturaldigital, 22 (top);
Peter Kim, 13; Pichugin Dmitry, 20; Podlesnyak Nina, 6; Rigucci, 8; Robert Elias, cover; Roman
Sigaev, 17; Sally Scott, 25; slavchovr, 24; Vera Tropynina, 16; VeryBigAlex, 10; Wally Stemberger, 18;
Paul Clarke, 4, 5, 12

Printed in the United States of America in Stevens Point, Wisconsin.
092010
005934WZS11

Down on the Farm

written by **Amy Houts**   illustrated by **Steve Harpster**

STONE ARCH BOOKS
a capstone imprint

HOW TO READ A GRAPHIC NOVEL

Graphic novels are easy to read. Boxes called panels show you how to follow the story. Look at the panels from left to right and top to bottom.

Read the word boxes and word balloons from left to right as well. Don't forget the sound and action words in the pictures.

The pictures and the words work together to tell the whole story.

Emily carried her suitcase and her toy horse to the car.

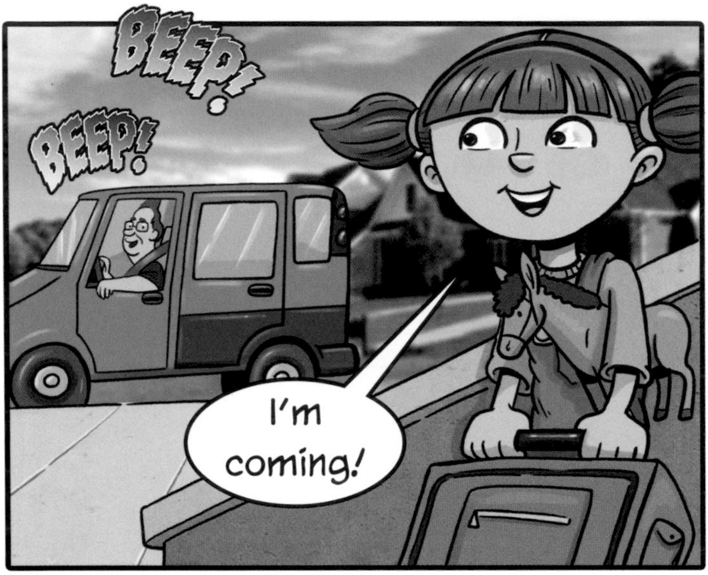
BEEP!
BEEP!
I'm coming!

Her dad was taking the family to a farm for the night. Emily couldn't wait!

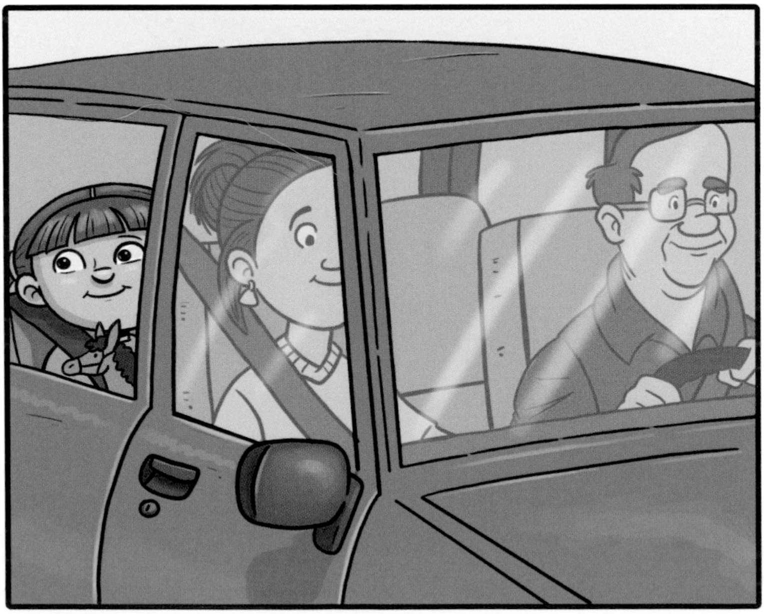

Emily had always dreamed of riding a horse.

Today, her dream would finally come true!

Lunch was set up on a picnic table. It was the perfect summer feast.

Emily watched the horses while she ate.

After lunch, it was time for a hay ride. Emily loved sitting on the hay bales.

Emily smiled as they toured the farm. It was so big!

Horses ran in the field.

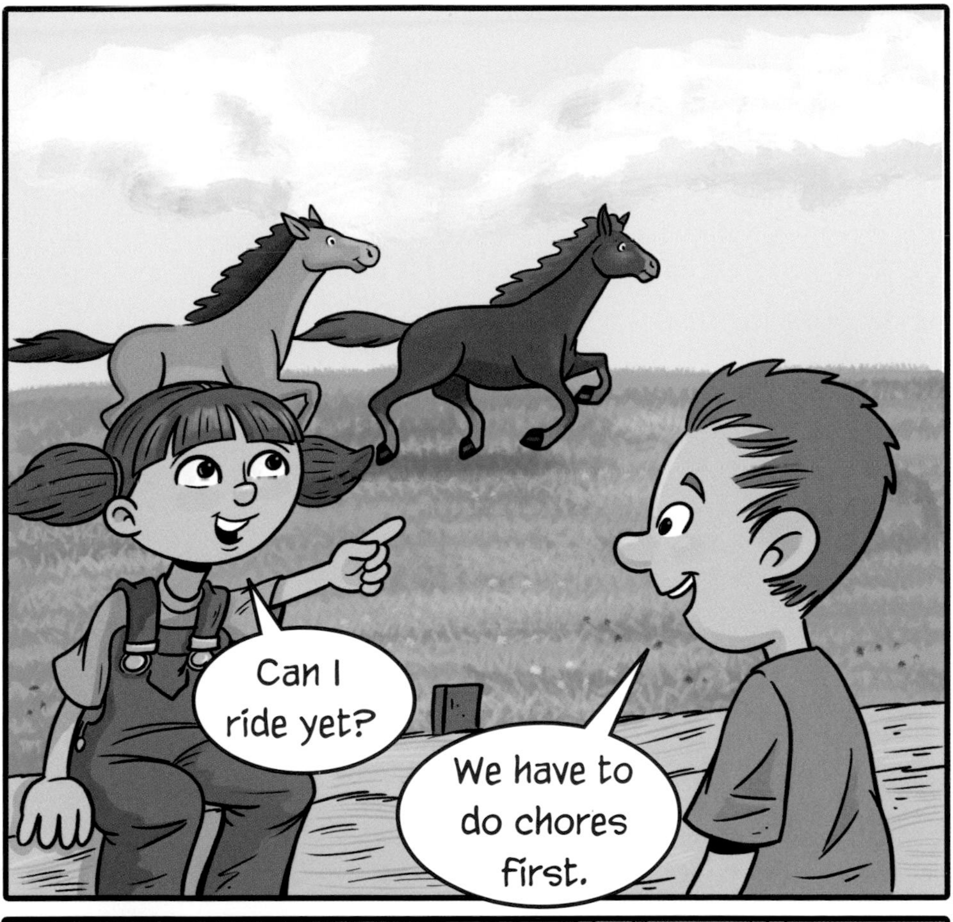
Can I ride yet?
We have to do chores first.

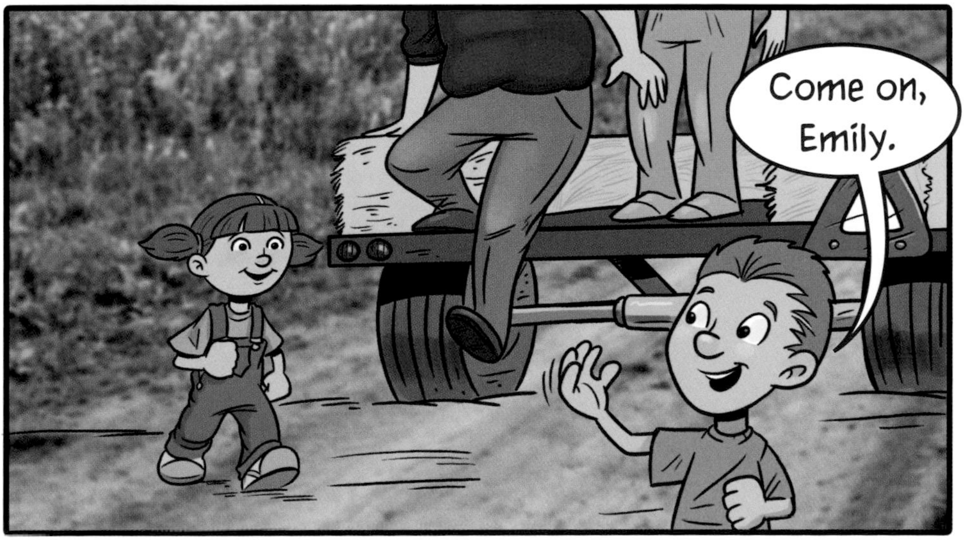
Come on, Emily.

First, Emily had to pick some corn. The corn stalks towered over her.

The mud stuck to her shoes like glue.

It took a long time to fill her bucket.

Aidan waited and waited for Emily to finish.

Next, they fed a calf. Emily held her nose.

Aidan gave Emily a turn to hold the bottle.

Then they walked to the pig pen. Aidan checked on the sows and piglets.

Aidan threw some feed to the chickens in the yard.
Emily threw some feed, too.

She held a soft little chick in her hand.

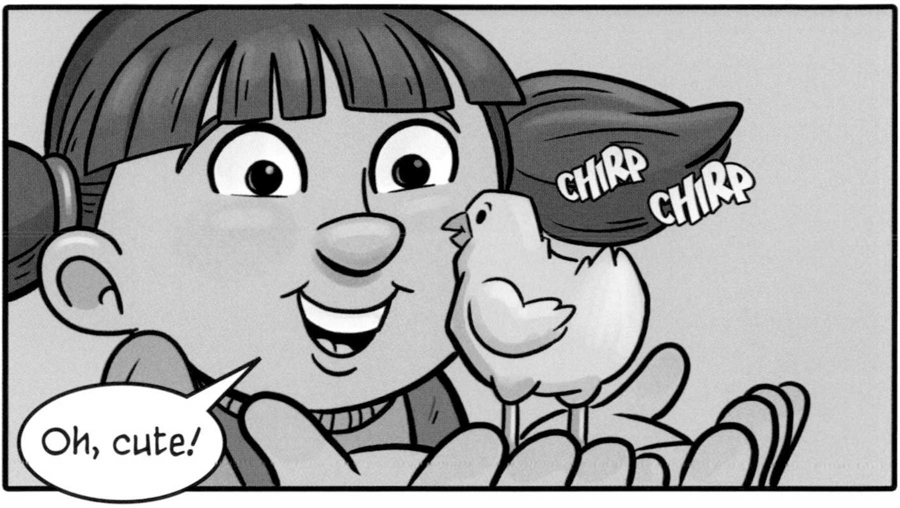
CHIRP
CHIRP
Oh, cute!

Emily yawned when she helped gather eggs.

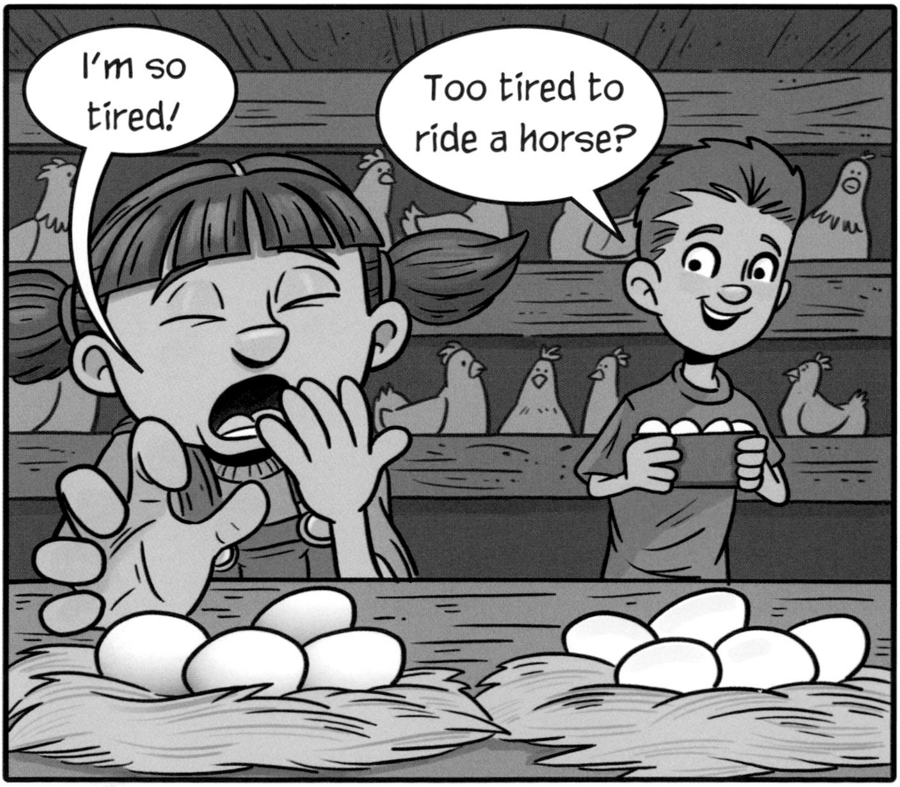
I'm so tired!
Too tired to ride a horse?

It was finally time. Emily was no longer tired.

Emily's dad helped her get on the horse.

After a quick lesson from Aidan, they were ready to ride.

They rode through the fields.

They rode to the river.

They rode for the rest of the afternoon.

21

After supper, Emily played with her toy horse in a warm bubble bath.

Then she got ready for bed.

She slept with her toy horse and dreamed of the next day.

Everyone would eat the eggs she gathered.

She would help feed the animals.

And best of all, she would ride again.

BIOGRAPHIES

AMY HOUTS and her family have lived in rural Missouri for the past 20 years. Her husband, Steve, grew up on a farm in northwest Missouri. Taking walks over the rolling hills of the countryside helps Amy think about new stories to write. Amy has two daughters.

STEVE HARPSTER loved drawing funny cartoons, mean monsters, and goofy gadgets since he was able to pick up a pencil. Now he does it for a living. Steve lives in Columbus, Ohio, with his wonderful wife, Karen, and their sheepdog, Doodle.

GLOSSARY

BALES (BALEZ) — large bundles of hay that are tied tightly together

CHORE (CHOR) — a small job that needs to be done often

MANURE (muh-NOO-ur) — animal poop used to help crops grow

SOW (SOU) — an adult female pig

TOURED (TOO-urd) — shown around a place

Emily's Farm Facts

I was super excited to visit a farm. Before I went, I did some research. You won't believe what I found! There are all kinds of unusual farms.

1. Ostrich farms. The birds are raised for their meat, eggs, feathers, and skin.

2. Fish farms. Some fish are raised for people to eat, while others are sold as pets. Some are even raised to be used as bait.

3. Tree farms. On tree farms, the trees are used to make many other products. New trees are always being planted.

4. Wind farms. On wind farms, wind turns big windmills. The windmills help make electricity.

I ♥ HORSES!

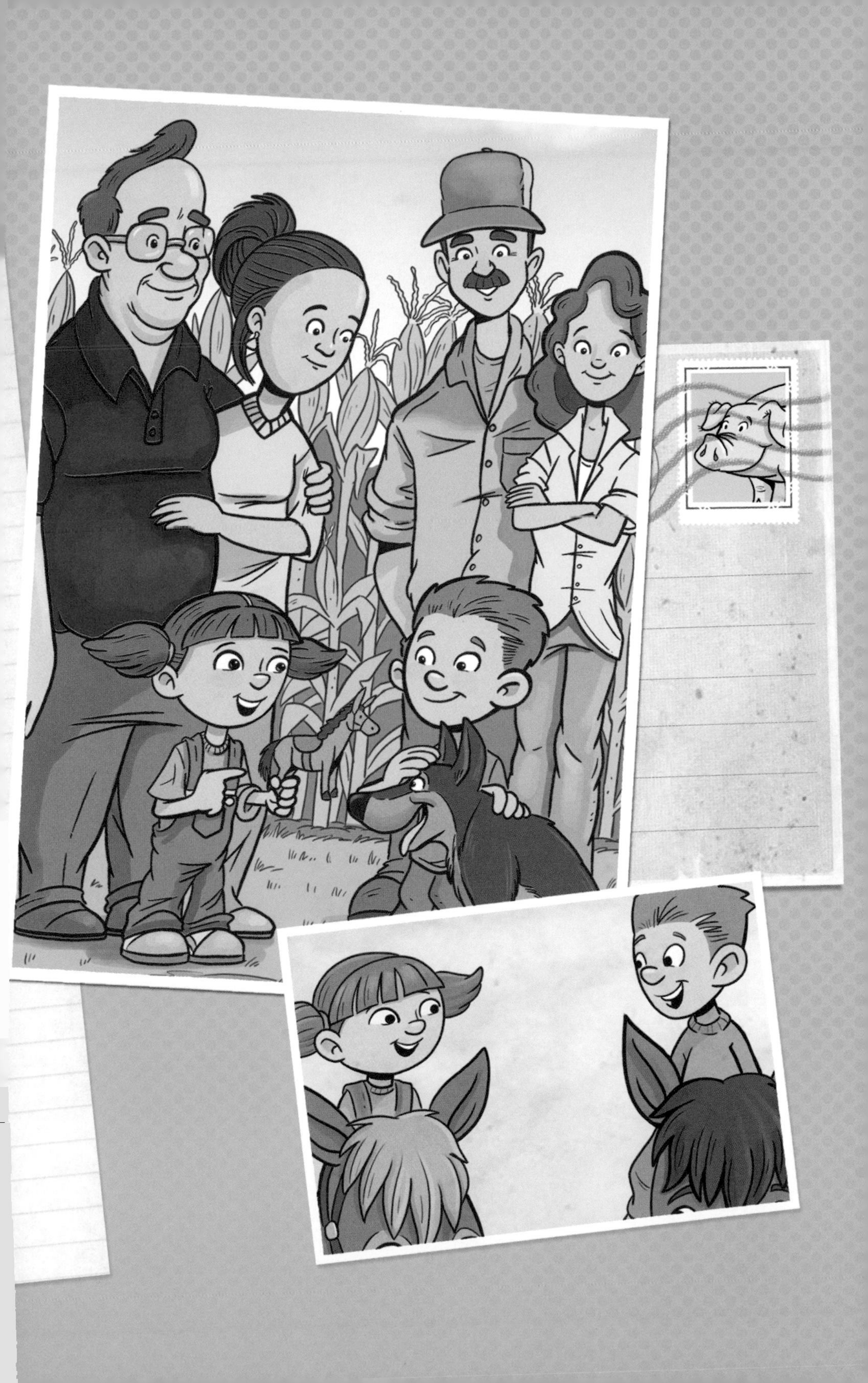

DISCUSSION QUESTIONS

1. Have you ever been to a farm? If so, what animals did you see? What crops were grown there?

2. Would you like to take a farm vacation? Why or why not?

3. The farm was very different from Emily's home in the city. How is your home similar to or different from a farm?

WRITING PROMPTS

1. There are different animals on a farm. Pick your favorite animal, and draw a picture of it.

2. Emily was excited about riding a horse. Make a list of three other things you can do at a farm.

3. Emily had to help Aidan with chores on the farm. Write a few sentences about the chores you do at your house.